GANGBANG SEX COLLECTION

EXPLICIT DIRTY EROTICA SHORT STORIES

BREANA KHOR

CHAPTER 1

"IN A DAY'S WORK"

AS SHE OPENED her mouth to take another cock between her lips, twenty-one year-old Heidi Kurth's mind flew back to earlier that day, back when she'd been sent to fill in for a sick colleague.

"You want me to do what?" Heidi stared, silver gray eyes incredulous.

"Scott's sick and we need someone to interview the new third baseman for the Panthers," the editor repeated himself. "They should be finishing up the *Sports Weekly* photoshoot in a few minutes. Get a couple quotes; ask the questions I gave you."

Heidi bit back a retort and left the office, fuming. She raked a hand through her blue-black curls and grabbed her car keys. Traffic was against her so by the time she arrived, the players had already headed for the showers. She stood outside the locker room door, leaning against the wall and scowling as she waited. When fifteen minutes passed and no one emerged, she made up her mind. She had more important things to do than stand around waiting for some overpaid athlete to finally decide to appear.

"Fuck it."

She took half a dozen steps inside and stopped, frozen. She stared. She couldn't help it. The five hottest athletes she'd ever seen were standing on the far side of the room in various states of undress.

Actually, that was an understatement. Two wore towels. The rest had on nothing at all. Her gaze greedily devoured each one.

Amon Gilen was the one she'd been sent to interview. Orange curls, crystal blue eyes, and a lean body that was every inch as hard as it looked in his uniform. She took a moment to wonder what was under his towel before moving on to the next one. Karsten Wheeler, the starting second baseman, had dark brown hair and eyes as blue as the midnight sky. He was more muscular than Heidi would've guessed. Iggy Kimura had burgundy hair, storm gray eyes, and a long, thick cock that seemed out of proportion with his five feet, six-inch height. She licked her lips, imagining how it would grow in her mouth. Beni Oates was the catcher. Rust-colored hair, topaz eyes, and a firm ass that Heidi had the sudden urge to bite. And then there was Tait Oldham, the oldest player at thirty-two. Thick ebony hair, nut-brown eyes, and an all-over tan.

He spotted her first and turned with the attitude of one who knew how good he looked naked. "Lose your way?"

The other men turned towards her, none of them making an effort to cover themselves. "I'm filling in for Scott Billa, the sports reporter for *The Herald*. I'm supposed to interview

Amon Gilen."

She still wasn't entirely sure how it started. It just seemed like one minute she was standing there, trying not to gape like an idiot, and the next minute, she was down on her knees, a cock in either hand and one in her mouth. Time became meaningless, a blur of images and sensations that she gave herself over to without a moment's hesitation. After all, how often did a chance like this present itself?

Iggy knelt behind her, his tongue working its way into her asshole as she swirled her tongue around Karsten's cock, feeling it swell in her mouth. She took more of the velvet steel as Iggy's tongue pushed past the tight ring of muscle.

Amon's fingers tightened in her hair as he forced his cock further into her mouth. She relaxed her throat muscles, letting him slide down her throat. When Beni shoved his fingers into her pussy she moaned, the sound muffled.

Tait was the first inside her, bending her over one of the benches and taking her from behind. He slid in slowly, each inch stretching her in a deliciously agonizing way. She pleaded with him to move faster and he responded by motioning for Iggy to silence her. She eagerly parted her lips, stretching them wide around the thick shaft as Tait's thrusts pushed her forward until the head of Iggy's dick bumped against the back of her throat.

Her pussy was dripping as Karsten moved beneath her, his hands on her hips. When she felt Beni behind her, his tip nudging against her ass, the heat that had been pooling low in her belly exploded and she'd begged him to do it. The initial penetration had burned, mingling with the thousands of other sensations coursing through her body. Karsten's cock pumping up into her. Iggy's mouth on her breasts, scraping his teeth over her sensitive flesh. Amon's hand on her other breast, rolling her nipple between his fingers. Tait's cock in her mouth, the salty taste of his pre-cum thick on her taste buds.

Pleasure coursed through her, overwhelming her, as the two men alternated thrusts, filling and emptying her in a steady rhythm that soon had her writhing. Her cries filled the room as Tait slid his cock from her mouth. Her muscles quaked as she came, tightening around the men inside her, tipping them over the edge.

She was still trembling when they pulled out, her body twitching. She whimpered at the sudden loss, but it lasted only a fraction of a moment, and then Tait was there. He rolled her on top of him and slid inside in one smooth motion. She swore as her over-sensitized skin struggled to absorb more than it could handle. When Iggy buried himself in her ass in one swift thrust, she screamed, limbs going rigid. One climax rolled into another as the men continued their ministrations, not stopping even as her body went limp, her eyes rolled back in her head.

Heidi didn't know how anyone could take so much plea-sure and not combust. Electricity raced along her nerves, synapses firing so rapidly that she could almost hear the crackle. The world narrowed down to hands, lips, tongues, pussy, ass, cock, and the slide of skin on skin. Every smell and sound blurred together until the world detonated and everything went white.

A low, masculine chuckle broke through the darkness. "I think we broke the reporter."

"Not broke," Heidi felt a surge of pride that she could speak. She struggled to lift her eyelids. A ring of faces stared down at her. "Not broken," she insisted. "Just thoroughly fucked."

The entire group laughed this time and she managed to sit up. Her entire body ached and she knew she'd be sore tomorrow, but it had been well worth it. "Any chance I could use your shower?"

Tait stood and extended a hand. "I think we could all use one, what do you say?"

Heidi grinned as he helped her to her feet. "Sounds good, but when we're done, I still need that interview."

CHAPTER 2

"JOURNEY OF DESIRE"

THE THREE MEN at the end of the trail were all watching her with the same half-predatory gleam in their eyes. Twenty-one-year-old Sharon Geyer shivered as her boyfriend put his arm around her waist, fingers splayed on her hip in a possessive manner. He leaned close and whispered in her ear.

"Just say the word and we'll go home."

Sharon hesitated for a moment, the cool spring breeze playing with her persimmon-colored curls. Deacon would turn around and leave, she knew, if she said it, and there'd be no judgment, no recriminations. But, she'd always know that she'd been the one to back out first. And, if she was to be entirely honest with herself, when Deacon had told her about his cousin and his two friends, something inside her had tightened. Sharon looked up at her twenty-two-year-old boyfriend, her pale blue eyes locking with his steel blue ones. The heat she saw there solidified her choice. She nodded. "Let's do this."

Deacon Lehane grinned and gestured towards his nine-teen-year-old cousin. The moment Anderson Austin stepped forward, his platinum blond hair far lighter than his cousin's hazelnut locks, the mood shifted.

"Tie her up," Anderson's ultramarine eyes had darkened from their near purple to almost black. "Vance, take care of her clothes."

The two men who stepped towards Sharon were both tall, muscles clearly outlined under their t-shirts. The one Anderson called Vance had mahogany hair and dark gray eyes. The expression in the other man's moss green eyes made Sharon swallow hard. When his hands closed on her arms, his knuckles brushed against the sides of her breasts and she tensed, nerves stretched tautly.

By the time the men marched Sharon up to a large oak tree, Deacon had settled onto a rock at the edge of the path. Sharon faced him, the body already starting to tremble. The ropes hanging from one of the tree branches hadn't helped. She bit her lips to hold back a protest as Vance yanked her t-shirt over her head.

"Gale, get her shorts," Vance's voice was soft.

The sandy-haired young man did as he was told, tossing the garment to the side. While kneeling, he wrapped a rope around one ankle, tying it just tight enough before moving to the next one. Sharon whimpered as Vance trussed up her arms, leaving her body, clad in only a white cotton bra and panties, spread in an X.

"Anderson," Deacon handed his Swiss army knife to his

cousin. "What do you say we all get a look at that gorgeous body?"

The slice of metal through cloth was nearly deafening to Sharon and she fought the urge to struggle. The remnants of her undergarments fluttered to the ground, baring full, heavy breasts tipped by caramel-colored nipples that hardened almost immediately, and exposing a bare, newly shaved pussy. She felt the heat rise in her cheeks.

"Gale," Anderson handed over the knife.

The bigger man took it without a word. He paused, letting his hungry gaze travel over Sharon's body before stepping off the trail. A few silent minutes later, he emerged with a thin, peeled switch.

"Fuck," Sharon whispered the word, eyes wide.

Gale handed over the knife but kept the branch, moving to stand in front of Sharon.

She heard it whistle through the air but was still unprepared for the sudden sting on her breast.

She yelped, flinching back, the ropes chafing against her wrists. Before she'd fully recovered, the switch connected with her other breast, and this time she swore. Red stripes marred her pale flesh as Gale continued to flick out his wrist, snapping the switch against her body. And yet, even as her breasts burned, and throbbed, with every new blow, Sharon's pussy throbbed for a different reason.

Vance's voice broke the relative silence. "Fuck, she's dripping."

"Why don't you clean her up?" Deacon kept his eyes locked on Sharon as he pulled his cock from his pants. "And Gale, think you could soothe her tits?"

Sharon nearly sobbed in relief when Gale dropped the branch. The sob turned into a full-out cry when two large hands mauled at her breasts, his fingers pinching at her overly sensitive nipples.

Second, Vance was suddenly between her legs, tongue running up the inside of her thighs. "Anderson," Deacon's eyes flickered towards his cousin for a brief moment before returning to

Sharon. "Would you like to show my girlfriend what you like to do?"

Sharon knew she should've felt something other than desire when Anderson stalked her, but she was having a difficult time forming any sort of coherent thought. When Gale's lips closed over her nipple, the last remaining remnants vanished and she was reduced to trying to handle the myriad sensations assaulting her.

Vance's mouth reached the apex of her thighs, his tongue eagerly lapping up her juices. He ran the flat of the thick muscle across her entrance and up to her clit before changing tactics and circling the little bundle of nerves with the tip of his tongue. As he began to dart his tongue into her pussy, Gale switched breasts.

So distracted by the pair was she that she didn't realize that Anderson had walked behind her until his hands were on her ass, pulling apart her cheeks. The moment the tip of his tongue breached the puckered ring of muscle, Sharon keened, her body stiffening.

It didn't stop, didn't even fade. The energy and pleasure washed over her, one wave rolling into the next. The tide came into the shore, crashing against the rocks. A wildfire fueled by dry summer winds, unable to be quenched by the rains. A cacophony of sensation orchestrated by the most talented of participants, each one playing her body like a fine instrument.

Her body went limp, and still, they continued, heedless of the ropes rubbing against her already tender wrists, of the pain starting in her shoulders as they held her weight. Through half-lidded eyes, she was vaguely aware that all three men were stroking themselves and that Deacon was standing, walking towards her. Even as she felt the warm, sticky liquid spurt over her legs, Deacon's arm was there, around her waist, relieving the pressure on her shoulders, ordering the men back.

She nearly sobbed in relief as the trio of mouths moved away and, a moment later, she felt the ropes around her wrists and ankles give way. She wrapped her arms around her boyfriend's neck, clinging to him as he half-carried a few steps until she felt the rough bark against her back. She let her forehead fall against his shoulder, barely aware that he was lifting her, wrapping her legs around his waist.

"Fuck," she wailed as Deacon buried himself in her overly sensitive pussy. Spots danced in front of her eyes as he thrust into her. She dug her nails into his shoulders and his hips jerked. He swore, shoving himself deep inside as he came.

They slumped to the ground together, Deacon on his

knees and Sharon on his lap. He nuzzled his nose against the soft spot just under her ear and then brushed his lips across her temple as he tightened his arms around her. "That was amazing."

Sharon made a noise of assent, unable to form an actual word. Deacon's chuckle rumbled through his chest and she raised her head. The trio of young men stood behind him, looking down at her.

"Sharon, I'd like you to meet my cousin Anderson and his friends, Vance and Gale," Deacon brushed back a sweat-dampened curl.

"Nice to meet you," Anderson grinned. "I've got to say, I think family holidays are going to be a lot more interesting now."

"Anderson," Deacon's voice was mildly chiding.

"It's okay," Sharon managed to speak. "I tend to agree with him." She winked and snuggled closer to him. "And I think we need to invite all three of them to play more often."

"Sounds good to me," Deacon glanced back at the trio. "What do you think?"

"I think my parents have a fully-stocked cabin about half a mile from here and we all have a three-day weekend," Gale's eyes were nearly glowing.

Deacon looked down at Sharon who immediately nodded.

"You're going to have to carry me," she wrapped her arms around his neck. "I don't think my legs are going to work for a while."

With a laugh, Deacon got to his feet and cradled Sharon against his chest. After all, she'd need even this small rest. It was going to be a long weekend.

CHAPTER 3

COLLEGE FRESHMAN GANG BANG (COLLEGE/CAMPUS/ DORM ROOM)

THE FRESHMAN YEAR of college can be a tough time for any student. When you are a geek that everyone else makes fun of, it's even worse. Frank House was scared of moving away and going to college. He had got in based on his grades and was being placed in all honors classes, which was a red flag to potential tormentors. His father had said that this was a new chapter in Frank's life. Frank packed his stuff and made the move to college. His dad had given up on his dreams. This was the chance for Frank to destroy the mold and to do things a whole new way.

Frank arrived at his dorm room and took one look around; it was not what he had expected. He had his own room. This also meant that he would not be distracted by anything that would keep him from his studies. He had been invited to a party as a welcome to school that was being held by one of the frat houses. Frank was not the party type but he saw it as a great chance to meet a few of the other students.

. . .

Frank was walking around, getting a feel for the type of people that were on campus. There were all types - jocks, frat boys, bimbo girls, and a few like him scattered all over the campus. One girl happened to catch his eye. For some reason, he was attracted to her and could not take his eyes off her. The girl introduced herself as Heather. She was a history major and she had transferred from a college in Iowa. This seemed too good to be true; he was originally from Iowa and had never known anything past the state borders until he moved to Montana. They went back to her room where they sat down and had a few drinks. Frank had made a few friends before the party. After a few drinks, he called them over to Heather's dorm.

He had talked the girl into a gangbang. He and about three of his friends wanted to fuck her until they could not cum anymore. Heather had mixed feelings on this, as she had never been in this type of arrangement. The other side was that Frank had no experience either and had taken all of his lessons from the porn movies that he had watched. This meant that he never had been with a woman and had never felt the inside of a pussy. Frank and Heather already gotten started by the time the others had arrived. Heather was a little more experienced.

A little while later, the rest of the people showed up and joined the action. Heather, when it was all said and done, had a cock shoved into every hole at the same time. In a couple of holes, she had more than one cock that was riding her at the same time. The one thing that seemed amazing was that she was able to take all of these inside of her. She laid there and just got into the act of being pounded from all angles. Frank was the first one to pop and aimed his cock at the tits and face of Heather. The load that sprang from his cock was white, clumpy, and thick. There was also a very large amount of cum that had been included with the shot he was placing onto her tits. Heather had been working the edge of her clit over while this was taking place. The sensation of the cum hitting her tits was immense and it caused her cunt to erupt, even though she had a cock shoved into her cunt. It did not stop the eruption that occurred within her, taking many she was with by surprise.

The rest of the loads went in a number of places, including a couple that were placed in her eyes. The rest of the night the people that were all part of the entire scene took turns pounding Heather and giving her a load of their cum. Heather looked to be as happy as any woman that had been pounded. Frank left her dorm room with the satisfaction that he had attained one of the rites of being a man

The rest of the semester Frank spent being the idol of the campus. Men wanted him for his brains and women wanted him for his body. The two put together was all he needed to feel like he was on top of the world. As long as he was in demand, he would not have to worry about being made fun of and would remain on top without question.

CHAPTER 4

DELICIOUS BANANA SPLIT

I ALWAYS WANTED to experience an orgy. It excites me to even think about it. And tonight I vowed to myself that I would be in one wild, sex orgy before the night is over. So here I was, dressed up with a teeny-weeny tube blouse and a micro-mini to get the words across before I even opened my mouth.

I looked around the bar and saw these 3 young men. They were obviously having a grand time. They were in their early twenties and they were dashing, full of vibrancy and life. I imagined all of them exploring my body and I trembled with excitement.

I couldn't wait any longer so I stood and walked boldly to their table. "Mind if I hang out with you guys?" I smiled my sweetest smile.

They were startled at first, unable to speak, but was only for one interminable minute. Perhaps, they saw I could be a prized item; my father used to say that I would surely break many men's hearts.

"Sure," the tallest man made a room for me beside him. I noticed he had a growing erection.

I sidled up to him and made no pretense of hiding my creamy thighs when my mini skirt hiked even higher.

He smiled, his face flushed with lust, "I'm Ken," his hands dropped to my thighs instead of shaking my hands. That was what I wanted and I spread my thighs wider as he started caressing them. The other two men stared fixedly at us, seeming to have been hypnotized.

My right hand shot to Ken's crotch. He shuddered, more aroused with my touch. In the semi-darkness, I could feel that he was as huge as a horse's, and my pussy quivered with eagerness. How good it would be to feel that hard, hot dick inside me, I thought.

I stood and seated myself between the two men. "I'm Jeff," he said as my left hand dropped to his dick to fondle it underneath his jeans. He was hard as a rock as well, and his face was suffused with passion. Jeff bent to kiss me as Ken's fingers crept upward inside my skirt.

The third man watched as he hyperventilated and wanted some piece of the action. They were getting wild, so I whispered, "Can we go somewhere more private?"

They needed no further prodding as Ken gripped my hands to whisk me into his car. The two men trailed behind their faces beet red with enthusiasm. Wow, they would surely fuck me until I would be completely satiated.

While Ken was driving, I continued caressing his tumescent shaft. He groaned and told me to stop or we'll end up on the roadside. But I knew it was taking him a Herculean effort to concentrate on his driving; he wanted me to suck him.

I scrambled to the backseat of the car and open myself wide for the other two men. Jeff was already massaging his erect penis when I wiggled between them. He ripped my blouse open and grabbed my luscious tits in his hands, as he directed my face to his red, swollen dick. He groaned wildly as I licked the crown of his dick and ran my tongue up and down his manhood.

The backseat was cramped but the third man managed to lift my butt up, get rid of my undies and started running his tongue on the lips of my pussy. The three of us were making delighted noises in between the slurping sounds that Ken cursed under his breath. He wanted to take part in the action.

The sweet, delicate folds of my labia were receiving the most exquisite sensations I had ever experienced, and it was driving me crazy as I took Jeff's penis full into my mouth. He was so big, that I nearly choked. I sucked his penis while my mouth went in and out of his shaft. He was writhing and grunting in unbridled ecstasy.

I stopped now and then to savor the tongue deliciously exploring the innermost recesses of my pussy. Then the car stopped and Ken carried me like a rag doll and deposited me onto the carpeted floor of his living room.

As soon as I was on the floor, they literally attacked me like they had been deprived of sex for several days. Ken discarded his jeans on the floor and shoved his throbbing dick into my mouth; I sucked his huge dick and played with his balls with my fingers. The third man was pulling my butt upwards so he could penetrate me from the back. Not to be outdone, the third man stood beside Jeff and they alternated shoving their dicks into my welcoming mouth.

I was on all fours, with the two men in front of me and Ken thrusting his pulsating penis into my slick pussy. My wildest dream of being in an orgy has finally come true. I pushed my buttocks against Ken as our hungry groins slapped against each other.

Then Jeff, positioned himself below me, his face

upturned towards my pussy, as he licked my clitoris while Ken fucked me harder and harder. I was moaning and crying wildly as my arousal heightened. I momentarily stopped sucking the third man's dick, and he was infuriated.

Jeff grabbed me by the waist amidst the protest of the two men and set me on the couch. He sat on it and carried me to shove his dick into my pussy. I cried when the friction of his dick going in and out of my pussy penetrated every nerve of my body.

Ken was at my back forcing my body to flatten against Jeff, to expose my ass. He then mounted me from behind inserting his dick into my anus. I was surprised but thrilled to experience what I had been dreaming of very often. He spat into my anus as he slowly penetrated my tight anal opening.

My mouth was sucking the third man's penis, while Jeff fucked my pussy relentlessly, and Ken has started going in and out of my ass. The sensation was beyond words; my body was ready to explode with all my nerve endings at the peak of unending stimulation. I gasped aloud when Ken pounded his dick into my backside as Jeff fucked me harder and faster in my pussy.

Suddenly, a trigger from my groin reached its peak as I moaned and shuddered as my orgasm came in one gigantic explosion. Jeff still kept pounding my pussy that I came again, with pure ecstasy that I clung to him, as Ken was still going in and out of my anus. Then I came for the third time as Ken and the third man grunted wildly as they squirted almost simultaneously their semen into my body.

What a mind-blowing sexual experience that was.

CHAPTER 5

MOVING IN/MOVING OUT

MOVING IN/MOVING OUT (THE MOVERS)

THE OUTLINE of Sam's cock gives its size away. It was expected that it would be large, as are the cocks of the three other black men in the apartment. Four Negros, Sam, Trey, Levi, and Saul all work for the same removal company, along with Lando, Rocky, and Luis, three Hispanic brothers. The seven were not all needed for this part of the process, her apartment was not big enough to need so many hands. It was just that Tanith had very heavy things, and so they all needed to work together to get these large furnishings up the dozen-plus flights of stairs that got them to Tanith's new condo.

She watches them for a minute, catching their breaths before following her instructions regarding placement. But Tanith is distracted by the fact that every single one of these men, all under twenty-five, all sported very large cocks, complimented by ripped torsos. She can't help but be overwhelmed by the testosterone that has completely filled the air in her space. Her nipples respond not just to the sight of the snow falling just outside the large living room windows, but to the fact that all of a sudden it occurs to her that she has a deep desire to be fucked. She can't imagine how this can happen though, given the fact that all the men seem to see when they look at her is the *boss*.

At thirty, Tanith isn't inexperienced, or unaccustomed to getting what she wants. This is how she landed the job that got her this amazing apartment anyway, and she has always been able to manipulate people and situations in order for her to get what she wants. What she wants right now is in front of her and all around her, but for the first time, she is unable to get herself to do what she needs to do to get the ball rolling. There seems to be a rapid progression of time as she watches them move around the space, getting hotter, and sweatier. In the hopes of distracting herself from her carnal desires, she gets actively involved, moving what she can, placing tinier items on larger ones that have finally found their spot. Soon she too is sweating, and her gym sweats are discarded for a tank and shorts.

Tanith tries to adjust a mirror in the dining room that finally looks like a dining room and catches the men in the other room through the arches checking her out. And why wouldn't they be? She had lengthy legs, tanned and toned, a perky ass, flawless breasts, and a cropped raven mane that barely kisses her long, elegant neck. If she was a hot dude in his twenties she'd be checking herself out too. But now finally, she's getting the attention she's been hoping to get for a while. She capitalizes on the moment and lets her tank ride up to reveal her midriff. Final adjustments to the mirror and she catch seven gents adjusting seven rapidly hardening cocks.

The walk back into the living room is a slow one. Tanith has every man planted where they stand, hands firmly on cocks, tongues licking lips. She enters the space knowing that there might be a need for her to actually ask for what she wants. She hopes it won't get to that as she passes Sam first, then Saul. She is hoping that by the time she gets to the window someone will have made a move. She doesn't get to the sofa before all seven men have surrounded her and are staring at her as though she is a succulent roast ready for the carving. This is the look she has craved along with each one of their cocks. They move in.

Tanith's hands on the cocks closest to her let everyone know that it's a go. She is immediately descended upon, hands and lips finding every available part of her. She raises her arms as her top is removed, and steps out of her shorts and panties at the same time as four hands remove these. Someone, she doesn't see who removes her bra in one move, expertly. She drops to her knees as every man lets his cover-alls, already tied with the sleeves at the waist, drop to the ground, followed by their boxers. Seven solid cocks surround her, her hands immediately going for the two to the sides of her, left and right. They belong to Lando and Sam. Tanith pulls on the Latino to her left, the black cock locked in a firm right hand.

In front of Tanith are Luis and Rocky, long cocks protruding out before them. They step forward and guide their cocks into her mouth. She opens wide so that both dicks move into her with as much ease as possible. The men struggle against each other for a bit but eventually both cocks have managed a good few inches into her mouth. They fuck the beautiful mouth in unison.

Tanith enjoys the taste of the hot dicks, the feel of them moving against her tongue, filling the back of her mouth.

She can't bring herself to close her eyes despite her pleasure, the view of all the cocks around and inside her too good a sight.

Behind her are Trey, Levi, and Saul, all locked and loaded with twelve-inch ebony rods. Trey and Levi rub their dicks against the sides of her face, Trey having a more ambitious idea. He gets down on his knees and rubs his cock between Tanith's ass cheeks. He squeezes her perfect ass over his dick and thrusts forward without threatening to penetrate her hole. For the moment, the feel of her soft flesh is sufficient for his arousal. Everyone is pleased enough for any contact with the woman on her knees. Her flesh is soft, pale, and delicate; its smell is of flowers and potential sex. The moment is briefly suspended and then everyone gets into the real gist of what is about to go down.

With her mouth free she is helped to her feet. Her legs are parted and Trey is also on his feet. He still keeps his cock against her ass even though nobody else has their cocks in contact with her body. Then he is on his knees again and parting her ass cheeks, sending his tongue into her asshole and into her ass. Rocky and Luis are kissing her legs, Sam on his knees now in front of her and licking her cunt. Lando stands over Sam and kisses her lips and breasts. Levi wants in on some of the action but there just isn't enough of her for seven men at once. Tanith is moving in and out of lust-induced semi-consciousness and twice she almost falls onto Trey, Lando holding her up both times. The seven of them are incapable of concentrating on hauling her up and taking care of their own dicks at the same time.

They manage to get her to the couch, no time or experience between all of the men to have extended foreplay to anything else that has anything to do with anything other than their own dicks. What they want now is her pussy, dripping and perfect. Tanith gets onto the sofa, facing out of the window. She has her knees on the seat, her arms and head resting on the backrest of the gray leather. It's comfortable, even on her knees. The men start to line up behind her, a few making their way to the front so that her mouth can appease their cocks while her pussy takes care of the rest. Lando is first in her mouth, immediately fucking her deep and slow so that she doesn't gag despite the depth and thickness of his dick. Sam and Trey are behind him and next to him, waiting their turn.

Rocky sends his cock into her pussy first, his long thickness deep inside her from the back. His thrusts are not as gentle in her cunt as Lando is in her mouth. Rocky understands that he doesn't need to worry about satisfying her, that responsibility resting on the last cock inside her. He just needs to make himself cum so that Levi, edgy behind him already, can take over. Rocky fucks her fast and he fucks her deep. He gets so close to shooting that he shocks even himself and he pulls his cock from her. He throws a look at Lando who removes his cock from Tanith's mouth and then bends to whisper something in her ear. He then throws his eyes in the direction of the entrance hall where Tanith's bag sits on the writing-table. A minute later Rocky is handing out condoms.

As a male-to-male courtesy, Rocky is inside Tanith again, everyone else taking turns in her mouth. Rocky's break to fetch the condoms means that he works a little harder to get himself to where he was before the withdrawal. This extra stroking, the extra hard fucking does something unexpected, and no sooner has he started to cum, does Tanith's pussy starts throwing up its own juice. She has a massive orgasm thanks to Rocky's powerful thrusting and exceptionally fat cock. The other six let out a tense gasp as Rocky and Tanith let out satisfied moans. For a moment there is the fear that nobody else will get a ride. But as soon as Rocky pulls his cock from her she turns around and gives the others an inviting look.

Levi fills her wet cunt next. He too thrusts enthusiastically and works to bring himself to climax before she's worn out. Tanith braces herself against the backrest of the sofa and since she doesn't have a cock in her mouth to distract her, focuses on the cock in her pussy pounding her from behind. She circles her ass and gyrates so that instead of Levi's thick dark meat fucking her, she is the one fucking the shit out of the massive cock. The others are even more excited about getting inside her now. It takes half the time it took for Rocky to cum for Levi to shoot his load. Tanith really knows how to get a cock to the finish line, and with so many cocks in the room, all promised a turn, for the sake of her fragile, pink pussy, she can't leave such massive tools to their own devices.

Luis and Sam are next and fuck her respectively until she lets their cocks know that they've just had the pleasure of making the acquaintance of a significantly experienced cunt. They cum at about the same time as Levi. All the men who've shot their loads gather to one side, condoms sorted, and pull on their cocks for the rest of the show. Three cocks are left to be serviced, but by the look of things, Tanith's cunt is looking a little tender, the perfect pink of it an almost strawberry red now. Lando gives her much-needed relief. He parts her ass and sends a finger into it. He fingers her for a bit with one, then two fingers, moistening and preparing her ass. Then he gives Trey and Saul an instructing look before he himself gets his head under her so that he can lick her cunt better. Saul doesn't need to be asked twice and soon his cock is pounding away inside Tanith's ass while her cunt is repaired.

By the time Trey is in her ass Tanith's tiny rear has warmed up to cock and so she manages to take him for the same ride that Saul had to take himself while she adjusted. And just like with Saul, Trey shoots a massive load thanks to the tight hot space. Lando gets up once he moves and after testing Tanith's pussy with a finger to see the level of comfort, he sends his cock into her pussy, perfectly prepared by him, for him. He fucks her swiftly yet very gently while the others move around to her face again, watching the fucking while beating their meat. As soon as Lando starts to cum, and Tanith starts her final orgasm, the others wank themselves to fresh orgasms as well and shower Tanith in warm jizz while Lando finalizes work on her pussy. With the apartment sufficiently broken in, Tanith thanks her movers and has a very good first night's sleep...

ABOUT THE AUTHOR

Breana Kohr is an emerging erotica author of many erotica kinks and sub-genres. Be sure to check out other books and leave a review if this story got you hot!

Visit my blog at Breana Kohr's Blog

Join my newsletter for the exclusive Breana Kohr's Newsletter

Sign up for Free Stories from Xplicit Press Authors

Xplicit Press Author Updates

Like Xplicit Press on Facebook

Follow Xplicit Press on Twitter

Readers: I want to expand a few of the stories to see where the characters can be explored further. If there are any of the stories that you would like to read more about again, I'd love to hear from you!

Keep In Touch
Breana Kohr
info@breanakohr.com

www.ingramcontent.com/pod-product-compliance
Lightning Source LLC
Chambersburg PA
CBHW020815130626
46554CB00006B/2450